My Heart Will Stay

By
Jennifer Leroux

Illustrated by
Ry Menson

Dedicated to those who flew away
and to the loved ones with whom
their hearts will stay.

For my beloved mother, Elizabeth.
thank you for instilling in me your
gift of poetic writing. This book was
written to honor your amazing life and
the love that your daughters carry
with them every single day.

And to James McGarry & family.
Your incredible legacy will live
on forever in the hearts and
minds of those you've touched.
Fly high, white owl.

Little one all soft and snug,
come close so you
can feel my hug.

I'll keep you safe and
keep you warm;
I will shelter you
from any storm.

I'll teach you, protect you
and help you grow;
I will show you what you
need to know.

Then with a nudge you'll spread
your wings, explore this world and
try new things.

And sure as the light from the
first evening star,
I'll always be watching
from near or far.

My love will be with you
when we're apart;
no distance can change
what we feel in our heart.

And if the time comes
when I must fly away,
I promise you that
my heart will stay.

You are forever a part of me,
so near to you I will always be.

I might not be right
by your side;
but I’m still close,
I’ll be your guide.

You may be small but
you’re very strong;
my heart will be with you
your whole life long.

You'll rise and thrive
with each new day;
my eyes will be watching
as you find your way.

Eternal love surrounds you; go
stretch your wings.
Make the most of each day and
follow your dreams.

333

I'm proud of you my little one;
fly free, be brave,
shine bright as the sun.

Made in the USA
Monee, IL
06 April 2022